Santa's Lay

OCTAVIA JENSEN

Chapter One:
Daddy Christmas

How I ended up getting recruited as a slutty elf was beyond me, but the pay was good and the perks were even better. Eye candy, free sex toys, *and* I got to keep the outfit when I was done? It sounded like a sweet deal all things considered, so I agreed almost instantly when my friend Stella offered to hire me for the Christmas season.

However, in practice… showing up to work dressed like a hooker at a Keebler holiday party was strange. Sex shop or not, I found myself tugging at the thin green dress and the striped panty hose I was forced to wear and hoping I wasn't having a Janet Jackson-level wardrobe malfunction.

Unfortunately, I was.

"Lift and fucking separate," I hissed to

myself, hastily doing just that as I shivered in the cold November air. I patted my chest with a frown as the door opened so fast it hit me and knocked me back a few steps — but strong hands grabbed me to stop my fall. "I— oh."

"Sorry 'bout that," the sexiest Santa I'd ever seen said, helping me upright and staring at me so intently, I squirmed. "You good?"

"Fine," I lied. "You should slow down, though. Might hurt someone." Like me. I was someone, though the more I took in his perfect beard, bright blue eyes and the muscles bulging under that open red coat, the more I realized I'd probably just thank him if he hurt me. "So you're Santa?"

"Might be. You want to come sit on my lap?" He winked, biting his lip as he strolled past me and greeted Stella with a one-armed hug. "Didn't think you'd find a sexy elf on such short notice. Glad I was wrong, Stell."

The fucking accent. I couldn't place it, but I found myself slack-jawed and standing out in the cold like an idiot because of said accent — even after Santa took my best friend inside.

Reason caught up with me quickly and I darted in after them just in time to hear my name.

4

"…Hadley can."

"Hadley can what?" I asked quickly. "If this is about the lap thing… I'm not doing that." *Yes, I would, and I will, and I want to.*

Stella grinned a little too knowingly. "I was saying that if anyone can draw actu- al, real-life men in here, it's you. For a sex shop, our clientele is mostly women."

"Getting Daddy Christmas over here probably wasn't the right move if you want- ed to change that," I blurted out, then in- stantly turned on my heel and faced the other direction like I was looking around instead of hiding the redness in my cheeks. "Where do I go?"

"Daddy Christmas," he repeated. "Can we make them call me Daddy instead of Santa?"

Stella snorted. "No, Kent. We can't. Go sit, your giant body is in the way and I need to talk to Hadley without your ears near us." She crossed her arms and waited for him to disappear into the back, and then pulled me off to the side. "You look gorgeous, Had. I knew you would. Look at these candy cane dildos, though —I already bought you one, so don't worry about that."

I wished I could focus on the Christ- mas-themed sex toys, but I was mortified at myself. "Did I seriously just call him that?" I whispered. "Did that just fucking happen?"

Stella laughed like the asshole she was. "Yeah, it did. And he heard it and now he will never let it go. He's fucking gorgeous, huh?"

Her voice lowered more the longer she spoke, and I couldn't stop myself from nodding. "You said his name is Kent? Is he seeing anyone? Not that I think he'd see me, I mean… obviously he can *see* me, I'm a person, but… wow. Never mind. What am I supposed to do here? Just stand there and look pretty?"

"Oof, Had. You're a mess. Should he have come with a warning label?" Stella chuckled and tugged me along to start giving me a tour while filling me in. "He's single, worked here for almost a year. He's not what you'd expect. He's kind of a dork, honestly, but based on some of the toys he's bought here, he has a kinky side I'm not privy to. You're more his type than I am, so I'm sure he sees you. Just stand there looking pretty and the Santa photo op comes with a little gift that you'll hand out. Customer gets to pick between the dick bottle opener or the boobs. It's a great marketing concept. Our logo is on it and people use them at parties and such. I'm rambling now. What was the question?"

"Something about Daddy Christmas, I think. But I do not need that obsession in my life, so I'm gonna be a good little elf," I lied as Kent came back out. "I'm gonna go. Looks like we've got our first customers."

I smiled at the women walking in as I went to stand by him and pointedly ignored the way he spread his coat and beckoned them forward. They giggled to each other and tried to push the shortest one toward us, but she looked as embarrassed as I felt — I almost felt bad for her.

"Welcome to CeCe's Toys," I said, "Where everyone's naughty all year round."

The catchphrase made me feel ridiculous, but not as ridiculous as when that short little woman climbed into Kent's lap like she owned him.

"Hey there." Kent flashed a smile that had every woman in the room wet. "You been a good girl this year?"

"God fucking damnit," I whispered under my breath. That accent was going to be the end of me, I was sure of it. When they both turned to look at me, I grinned cheekily to cover it up. "Sorry. I coughed."

She blinked at me and rolled her hips on Kent's lap. "Yes, Santa. I've been a good girl."

"I don't believe you." His eyes darkened as his hands roamed up her thighs way higher than any Santa I'd ever seen. "Think you been a naughty girl. What do you think

Santa should do about that?"

Stella grinned from the corner of the room as she rubbed her thumb against her fingers, signaling how much money Kent was going to make her. I couldn't blame her for assuming that — the "spank me" that the girl moaned out had me thinking this was going to turn into a sex fest before we were done, and I could only imagine how much money he'd bring in then.

Hell, *I'd* have paid him if he promised to call me a good girl.

I brought my legs closer together and fidgeted with my nails until she was final- ly climbing off his lap and holding out her hand to me. "I'll take the dick."

"Um… I think that's something for Santa to decide, not me," I said slowly, but the look on her face made me think twice. "The bottle opener! Oh my god, I'm sorry. Here." I fished one out of the bowl and handed it to her.

"I'd take the other one if it was for sale… just saying." She winked at Kent and went back to her friends, and he laughed loudly as the next customer climbed up.

Kent charmed the pants off of her too, as well as their flamboyant friend that got a little too friendly with Kent's abs, but based on the look in his eyes he didn't mind it in the slightest. This Santa's sleigh was open to all, regardless of gender.

By the time break time rolled around, I had to let Stella know she'd need to order more dick bottle openers next time, because it seemed nearly every customer wanted a cock after sitting on Kent's lap.

The man himself approached me in the back room, leaning against the counter like we were old friends. "So, Hadley. You got a boyfriend or something?"

I fought the urge to ask him to say my name again, slower this time and preferably with his hand between my thighs. "Nope. I prefer to spend my holidays as lonely as possible. For… tradition," I deadpanned. "Can't go screwing up a seven-year streak."

"Wouldn't want that," he agreed, his face lined with amusement. "Mine are pretty much the same as yours, but I have an annoying brother and he has a fat dog to keep me company. Are you from around here? How come I've never seen you?"

"I've lived here all my life. I just don't normally have to come to the store here since Stella brings me toys like every week. Where are *you* from? I'm trying to place your accent."

"I don't have an accent." Kent grinned widely, revealing teeth so straight and white it was annoying. "What makes you think I have an accent?"

I let out a sharp breath and brushed my dark hair out of my face. "My ears, but… I'm sorry if that was offensive," I offered, but every part of me wanted to fuck with him now. "It's kinda hot, though. Accents, I mean. Shame you don't have one."

"Is it a shame?" His smile faltered slightly. "What's so hot about an accent? You're the one with the hot accent, bird."

"Did you just try to insinuate there isn't anything hot about accents and then tell me my accent is hot?" I pulled my bottom lip between my teeth with a smirk, then walked past him toward the door. "Get your shit together, Daddy Christmas. We're not done yet."

Chapter Two:
A Little Santa-sy

The rest of day one was torture. I'd never wanted to ride someone's face so badly before — and listening to him alternate between "You've been a naughty girl" and "Are you gonna be a good girl for Santa?" had me questioning things I never thought I'd question.

Namely… if I was into that sort of thing. Santa.

The beard, the red suit, the boots.

The answer was clearly no, despite the fact that I was laying on my bed and slipping my hand into my softest sleep shorts to play with my neglected clit. It wasn't for Santa — not the chubby one that shimmied down the chimneys of strangers and not the sinfully hot one with a not-accent accent, either.

Absolutely not.

I rubbed in a slow circle and forced myself to relax, to think about something else. Some*one* else. Like Dean Winchester from *Supernatural* or Michael Scofield from *Prison Break.* Maybe a little Geralt of Rivia.

… Okay, maybe all three.

My hand dipped lower and my legs bent and fell to the sides as I curled one fin- ger inside of myself, then two as my other hand snaked under my shirt to play with my nipple piercings. The thought of the three of them bending me over Dean's Impala and having their way with me put me exactly where I needed to be, right up until all three of those bastards suddenly had Santa hats and thick, black belts.

"What the fuck," I whispered, stilling my hand and catching my breath. "Go away. I don't have a thing for Santa. That's not real."

I squeezed my eyes shut tighter and forced them back into the beautiful specimens I knew them to be, then continued bringing myself closer to the edge. I could feel how wet I was, how each swipe of my thumb over my clit made me gasp and arch my back, and I started to relax into the feeling until the Impala turned into a sleigh and Scofield grew a huge, white beard.

"For the love of god."

JENSEN

Giving up sounded like a good idea, but I glanced around my room to remind myself that I was alone. No one could see me, and no one could hear the thoughts running through my mind. If I wanted to have one, tiny little fantasy about Santa just to get it out of my system, who would ever know?

I would, but that wasn't the point. I had a list a mile long of fantasies I liked to pretend I didn't have. What was one more?

"Okay, Santa. You win."

It took all of two minutes for the previous fantasy to disappear entirely and replace itself with one of Kent. Full Santa outfit — not that his Santa suit was anything more than red pants and an open jacket — short, neatly-trimmed beard and ice blue eyes.

"You've been a naughty girl."

My toes curled.

"Wouldn't you rather be my good girl?"

"Yes," I hissed, flinging the sheet off of me and snatching my vibrator from my nightstand. My hands wouldn't be enough for this but I was too impatient to get one of my many dildos. I needed release fast, before I talked myself out of it.

I moaned as I held that vibe to my clit and closed my eyes again, bringing Kent back to the forefront. It wasn't hard to remember the way he'd gripped the waists of those lucky enough to sit on his lap —

13

the way he growled when they squirmed, grinding on him like they'd get him to take them home. The way that coat covered just enough to make me curious. The abs it revealed that I wanted to lick, to drag my tongue down until I was lower, right between his thighs and sucking him off right there in the middle of the store. I wanted those hands around my neck, gripping my ass and spreading me open, pinning me to any fucking surface we could find —

I came with him and that fucking Santa suit on my mind. My thighs were shaking and my heart was beating so fast I had to sit up for a minute, but I was too irritated and embarrassed at myself to really notice.

Santa Claus? Really?

No, I reminded myself. Not Santa. Kent. But maybe that was worse.

~

I nearly called off on day two, but Stella would've killed me, so I sucked it up and forced my tits back into that tiny dress. If I spent a little more time on my hair and makeup, no one needed to know but me, just like no one needed to know I'd finally shaved my legs for the first time in almost two weeks.

JENSEN

It was winter; I was cold.

The store was still void of customers when I got there, and I tried my best to ignore Kent's existence as I filled the basket with the bottle openers and straightened out the North Pole's set. The Christmas trees and little village were adorable, which was a stark contrast to where we were and the Santa that was sitting on that throne, but I couldn't deny that it was picturesque.

Stella's voice startled me just as I was fixing the church. "Fidget much?"

"It wasn't straight," I lied. "I'm not fidgeting."

"None of us are straight, Had. It's 2021. Straight people are a myth, huh, Kent?"

"What?" he asked, walking over to get in on our conversation, and I tried my hardest to look at anything but him. "What's a myth?"

"Straight people."

"Oi, don't say that like you're the one that came up with it. You didn't even believe me at first," Kent argued, and the entire time he spoke, I could feel his gaze on me. "Why are you talking about it, anyway? Think you're straight, Hadley?"

I still wouldn't look at him. "No, but I also don't think they're a myth. Can we move on? I was talking about the village."

"You like my little village, eh? Took me

15

like two hours and all this woman said was it needed more snow. We got enough snow outside, don't you think?" Kent reached out to move the sign I straightened back to its original position. "That's part of the aesthetic, Haddy."

The nickname made my stomach flip. "Weird aesthetic. Is everything about you crooked?"

"Some things just a little." Kent winked and moved back to his throne, leaving Stella and I staring at each other like we couldn't believe what he just said.

"I was fine before you came. Y'know, knowing I'd never get to see his cock and accepting the few times he let me stare at his giant bulge, but now I'm not okay. I need you to fuck him and describe his cock in detail for me. Deal?"

"No, not deal. No deal. No." I shook my head vehemently. "I'm not getting in- volved with that mess. That's a recipe for heartbreak and I can't afford to gain twenty pounds of Ben & Jerry's. Some guys are just too hot to casually fuck."

"That's true." Stella sighed heavily and stared at him like she was having a wet dream right then and there about him. My suspicions were confirmed when he took a drink of water and she whimpered as some of it dripped down into his beard.

JENSEN

I snapped my fingers in front of her face to pull her attention back to me. "Stell! You're drooling. Literally drooling. Wipe your chin and go open the door… it's time for day two."

Chapter Three:
Candy Cane Dildos

Seven people sat on Kent's lap before I decided I needed a break. It was slower than the first day, which was good, but I couldn't help the jealousy coiling in my gut every time one of those random people got their picture taken with his hands somewhere on their body.

It was enough to make me wish Stella allowed drinking at work.

Instead, I headed for the back office and got some water, then tried to pep-talk myself into getting over my crush. Kent had *way* too many eyes on him, way too many choices, way too much charisma and sex appeal to settle down. I wasn't the type of girl who could handle competition like that — I just wasn't.

That bottle was half gone when I felt something poking me just under that flimsy, short dress. I gasped, spinning quickly and swatting Kent's chest when I saw him. "What the *hell* was that! And I thought you said it was crooked?"

"It's a candy cane, Haddy." Kent waved the striped dildo in front of my face with a shit-eating grin, then leaned in so close I could smell the peppermint gum he was chewing. "Got somethin' else on your mind? No lyin' to Santa, now."

I avoided eye contact like my life depended on it and lied through my teeth. "Of course not. You just startled me, that's all."

"Bet I did. Been thinkin' about something you said yesterday. Stella gives you new weekly toys? Which ones, exactly? For… y'know… science."

I stared at the ground but refused to be embarrassed by this part. "Whatever looks fun or vibrates hard enough to wake the neighbors. And admittedly some stuff I'll probably never use that I have for shock value."

"Shock some, maybe, but something tells me that's not the kinda man you want, anyway." He moved in closer, his finger gently tilting my gaze up to meet his. "Am I guessing right?"

"Um…" The eye contact had me clench-ing my thighs and trying to ignore the rush of lust and butterflies that raced through my body. "No. It's not."

He smiled, that finger traveling just a little further down my chest than most men would dare, and then he stepped back com-pletely. "Thought so. Seem to be guessing a lot about you correctly. Tell me somethin' I'd never guess."

"I like ducks." Of all the things I could've told him about myself, I'd chosen that one. Why? What possessed me to forget every-thing sexy about myself and go with some-thing that… boring? "They're… pretty."

"Ducks? Like… quack quack ducks?" Kent tilted his head and stared at me like he'd never seen me before. "That's fuckin' adorable."

"You're fucking adorable," I countered unapologetically. "Don't look at me like that, you'll upset your customers."

"Fuck the customers," he quipped. "Why do you avoid my eyes so often, Haddy?"

Telling the truth sounded like a bad idea — how was I supposed to admit that eye contact with him made me weak? That more than three solid seconds of it would unravel me? "Why do you ask so many per- sonal questions about your coworkers?"

JENSEN

"My Ma used to say I was a curious one. Guess you'd call it nosey around here?" Kent moved away though, not pushing me further as Stella approached us and started talking about work. I felt his eyes on me though, and every time I dared to look, he didn't shy away.

"So, I guess what I'm saying is that I need a picture of you two for the Facebook page. Hadley, go sit on his lap."

My mind went blank. "What?"

Kent bit his bottom lip and sat down with a chuckle, patting his lap for me and opening his arms. "Come on, little duck. Sit on Daddy Christmas' lap."

Every instinct I had told me not to for obvious reasons, but how was I supposed to deny them? It was for work, so I straightened my spine and stepped up onto the platform to sit in his lap.

Before my ass could even touch him his giant hands gripped my hips to pull me in, and all I could smell and feel was Kent. "There you go. Comfy?"

"Absolutely." My heart jumped into my throat as I tried to act like I wasn't soaking my panties just from the way his hands felt. I had a role to play, so I leaned back, wrapping one arm gracefully around his head and spread my legs. "This good, Stell?"

"Oh yeah," she grinned, messing with the

camera on the tripod and Kent squirmed slightly underneath me.

"This okay?" Kent whispered as he moved his palm to lay on my thigh.

I smirked, tucking my bottom lip between my teeth and hoping I was affecting him as much as he was affecting me. "Mmhm. Make 'em believe it."

"That's a good girl," he growled, adjusting his posture one last time before we relaxed into each other. After Stella took a few photos of us, he gripped my chin and forced me to look at him, signaling for her to continue. "Just playin' my part, Haddy. How you think they'd like it if I had you get on your knees?"

My breath caught in my throat and I squirmed, gripping the armrests and letting out a sound too close to a whimper. Every inch of me hoped that my eyes weren't giving me away like they always did. "Probably like you're teasing them, which… I suppose would be good for sales."

Kent hummed. "You're probably right. Maybe we'll save that for another day, yeah?"

His eyes darkened, but before I could respond, Stella's voice boomed next to us. "Those were fucking beautiful. You two have a lot of chemistry."

"I'm pretty, he's pretty, who's surprised?" I asked, more confidently than I felt. "Is that all you need? I should go refill the bottle openers."

"Yeah that'd be nice. There's already a line out there so I'll go get them situated. I'll text you both some of those pictures."

Stella walked off, leaving me in Kent's lap, and he made absolutely no move to let me go. "So you think I'm pretty, little duck?" His hands roamed a little higher on my thigh. "So are you."

The doors opened then, saving me from a response other than, "We should get back to work." I risked rubbing my ass on his crotch before sliding down and winking at him as I walked away — two things that surprised me and made me hope he'd chase me.

When he didn't, I sighed and filled up the basket, then checked my phone four times to see if Stella had sent the pictures yet before rejoining them on the floor. Unsurprisingly, Kent was openly flirting with a blonde woman, his hands touching the exact spots he just touched on me, and I fought the urge to slap them both.

This is why I didn't get involved with men like Kent.

I tried telling myself it was just a job, and that was the only reason he was touching them — but that only reminded me that I wasn't any different. His hands were on me for a photo op, nothing more.

The thought made me chuckle — I'd been ridiculous, but I couldn't exactly blame myself for wanting him; all I could do was get my shit together and stop acting like a lovestruck baby.

If only it were that easy.

Chapter Four:
Christmas Kicks

After another week of the same cat-and-mouse game, I needed a drink, so I practically begged Stella to come to our favorite spot with me. The Burning River Pub was always a good place to unwind without having to worry about getting attacked — and the fact that I lived right next door meant I could walk home if I got too drunk. I actively tried not to go anywhere else if I could help it.

She agreed quickly. I knew she just wanted to hear the details about me and Kent, but I wasn't going to remind her that there weren't any and risk her changing her mind. Instead, I winked at her the first time she brought him up and waited until we were sitting in our usual booth with drinks in our hand to break the news.

SANTA'SLAY

"You're going to be disappointed, Stell. Nothing's happened that you didn't witness yourself."

"Ugh! Why not? He obviously likes you, too. You should have seen his boner when you got off his lap last week. He tried to move the jacket to block it, but I had already seen it. What's wrong with a little no-strings-attached sex? You've never been opposed before."

"I've never been this attracted to some-one before," I countered. "You don't hit-and-quit a guy like Kent. But he's definitely the type of guy that'll hit-and-quit you, and that's not a dynamic I wanna touch with the Grinch's 39-and-a-half foot pole. I don't care how big certain parts of him grow."

Stella had the nerve to laugh. "I get it, I do. But it's pretty big… he showed me a toy that matched his size. How hammered are we getting today? Walk back to your place and watch Christmas movies or karaoke Christmas carols drunk? No wait… option three. We fuck those two friends over there and pretend we aren't picturing Kent in a Santa suit?"

I eyed them and tapped my fingers on the table. "Option four. We flirt with them, then sing bad karaoke, then go back and watch Halloween movies so I stop thinking about Santa."

"I like that plan. Let's see how many drinks we can get them to buy us." Stella slid off her barstool and strolled over to say hi to them, then tossed her head back my way before returning. "Easy as pie. Oh, now I'm craving pie. Why don't bars ever have desserts?"

I could see the men ordering us all drinks, but my incorrigibly stupid ass was busy checking my phone like Kent somehow osmosed my number. "Dessert bars exist, just usually not with alcohol and classic rock. Though, seems Burning River is on a Christmas kick right now, too." I set my phone down with a sigh and shook my head at her when she squinted at me, then turned my attention to the sevens in the corner as our drinks arrived. "They're not bad. Do you have a preference?"

"Ehh… no. Guess I'll take the bigger one if you're not picky. I'll pretend it's He- Who-Must-Not-Be-Named and maybe blow him in the bathroom." Stella shrugged and greeted them enthusiastically, then held up her drink to mine. "To a cold November night we probably won't remember?"

"There's a pun in there that I'm too lazy to find," I said, clinking my glass to hers and checking my phone one more time. "But yes, to that… thing you said before."

I turned toward the smaller of the two just

to emphasize and introduced myself, but I knew almost instantly that I wouldn't hook up with him.

"My name is Ricky. You're very pretty, Hadley. I feel like I might have seen you two here before." His eyes flicked to Stella who was already close enough to smell his friend Derek, and I didn't miss the way Ricky moved closer to me.

"Well, if you've been here before and you don't have any issues with your vision, I'd say that's a safe bet." I pulled the straw of my drink into my mouth with my tongue and looked up at him through my lashes. This was fun, nothing serious, and I needed to get some confidence back. "Tell me about yourself. You have two minutes to convince me you're the one I should be talking to. Go."

"Two minutes? Wow, that's a lot of pres- sure…" Ricky rubbed his hands together and then took a drink of his whiskey. "Al- right. I'm an accountant… wait, that's fuck- ing boring. I love Christmas… will you two stop staring at me? You're making it worse." He rolled his eyes and turned his atten- tion back on me. "I love to cook, especially for my girlfriend when I have one. I never make her pay, never had a one-night stand before and I told myself I never would. I respect women too much, and that's not a line. I have 5 sisters and my dad was never around, so I think I'm pretty good with lady stuff. I'm a catch, so if you're not in the mood to reach out and grab me, that's fine with me. I'll still buy your drinks tonight and enjoy your company. Is my time up, or should I talk about my cat?"

I slowly set my glass down. "I appreciate your honesty. You can talk about your cat if you want, but they're not my favorite and I'd prefer you just danced with me instead. It's been a while since I've been able to have fun with someone that didn't expect anything of me."

"I won't lie and say my fingers aren't crossed for it, but I take rejection well and I love to dance." He held out his hand with a soft smile, and I took it even knowing I probably shouldn't.

"I'm not here for a relationship, Ricky," I said firmly. "I don't think I was here for a hookup either. This will go a lot better for both of us if you uncross those fingers." I spun when we got to the dance floor and pulled him in by his shirt. "Can you do that?"

The look he gave me was familiar. It was the same look a man always had when I had him wrapped around my finger and he'd walk into traffic if I said I'd touch his cock later. It was a look I'd grown used to over the years, and despite his nod, I knew those fingers were superglued.

"I can do that, Hadley. Just don't punch me if I get a boner, haven't gotten laid in a while and you really are the most beautiful woman I've seen in a long time… at least a year."

"Thank you." I pulled him closer and danced a little slower, completely off-beat from the music. "You're smoother than I gave you credit for at first, you know that?"

"Am I? Never been called that, but I'll be sure my sisters put that on my headstone: here lies Ricky Morgan. Smoother than she gave him credit for. A great try-er." He laughed, resting his hand in a respectable spot on my back. "So, is there a lucky guy we're trying to pretend doesn't exist, or…?"

I hated the fact that Kent's face came to my mind. He had no right to be there; he hadn't earned that spot yet. "Or maybe I'm just a woman that doesn't want to be tied down."

"I can respect that. I like how you dance," Ricky spun me around again and pulled me back in. "Who needs a beat these days?"

"Not me," I laughed, then twirled him around instead. "Beats are as overrated as boyfriends. We make our own music."

"Yeah, we do." We both turned as Stel- la pulled his friend into the bathroom, and Ricky chuckled. "Lucky Derek. He's definitely not against a one-night stand."

I bit my lip as I watched him stare at the door. "If you were into it too, I bet she'd take you both. She's always wanted to."

He thought about it. Even if he denied it out loud, he *definitely* thought about rushing in there for a night he'd want to remember, but his hand pressed a little harder and he shook his head. "She's not you. I'd rather do this."

He was a fool, but a good fool, and I relaxed in his arms as we kept dancing. He'd find someone someday, and though I knew that someone wasn't me, I was content for the night.

Chapter Five:
Red Velvet Pants

While Ricky simultaneously made me feel good *and* like an asshole, he did nothing to help me forget about Kent. If anything, he just brought the man closer to the forefront of my mind — here I was, turning down the first genuinely decent man I'd met since the last Ice Age, and for what? Daddy Christmas?

Hell. I silently berated myself the entire drive to work, and walking in, I decided that I wanted Kent to want me as badly as I wanted him. The plan was simple — stuff down that needy little sub that kept making me blush and avert my gaze, and turn on the cockier, more confident part of me that recognized I was beautiful, powerful, capable, and a damn prize.

The problem was that the two were intertwined, and Kent kept trying to pull out the half I was trying to ignore.

"Good morning," I said brightly. "I brought more snow for your crooked, weird village."

"Morning." Kent didn't stop until we were only inches apart. "Thanks for the snow. I put a little piece of you in there... look."

He pointed toward the center of the village, and when I noticed the tiny plastic duck, my jaw went slack. "That's the cutest thing I've ever seen. Look at him, he's got a little scarf!" It took an extraordinary effort not to squeal, honestly. It's little beak and tiny webbed feet were so adorable that I had to work overtime to keep that cool composure I'd had when I'd walked in, but I had a sneaking suspicion that Kent could see right through me. "Where did you find him?"

"It was easy. Only went to like six stores." Kent grinned and poked my cheek softly. "The smile was worth it. You can have him, but not until Christmas is over. He makes the village better. His name is Quack... 'cause I'm very creative."

I turned to face him and stepped in a little closer. "You look like you'd be very creative," I said playfully. "And you work overtime to please people. Does that extend to all areas of your life, or just plastic duck hunting?"

"All," he said without hesitation, that

sinful hand dropping down and gripping my hip. "I please others before I even consider pleasing myself. My number one rule, little duck."

My stomach flipped. "Maybe that's why Stella's making more money than she ever has. You're certainly pleasing the customers."

"Fuck the customers," Kent said cheekily as he slid his palm a little further to the small of my back to pull me in closer. "Come to my place after work."

I shook my head slightly and flattened my palm on his bare, muscled chest, letting myself daydream for just a moment about kissing that spot instead. "I'm busy. I'm sure you'll find someone though; there's already a line of people waiting to come sit on your lap. All you have to do is open the door, and then who knows. Maybe you can actually fuck a customer, since you keep saying it."

The look on his face was unreadable as he stepped back, but if I had to guess, it was a mixture of disappointment and amusement. "Note taken, Haddy. Too soon. I'll keep working on you." He tossed a wink my way before heading toward the door, and I took a moment to catch my breath and steady my shaking hands.

"This is fine. I'm fine," I mumbled to myself. "I can handle this. I'm good."

JENSEN

I took my place by his throne again and played my part as a ton of women and a handful of men straddled him, whispered in his ear, and got their pictures taken being touched by him. I hadn't considered how difficult the job must've been for Kent, but watching the way his muscles repeatedly tensed had me almost feeling bad for him — and wondering how hard he was under those red, velvet pants.

By break time, it was obvious Kent was struggling. He didn't say a word as he disappeared to the back and Stella made her way over to check on me. "Last night was fun. Homeboy had the biggest load I've ever swallowed though. Think all huge guys come that much?"

She glanced around me to ensure we weren't being overheard, which just made me laugh.

"I've met some who haven't, so… no. But thanks for putting that topic in my head." I glanced toward the closed backroom door and bit my lip, then shook off the thoughts of Kent. "Ricky was nice. Husband material, though."

"Husband? Gross. We're too young for that. Twenty-nine is the new twenty-one, right?" She chuckled and shoved me slightly. "His friend was one-night stand material, but the world needs those too."

Kent walked back out, chewing something, and froze when he caught us staring at him. "What? Were you two just talking about me?"

Stella scoffed. "Not everything's about you and your abs."

"My abs, eh?" He grinned and made his way over. "You wanna touch? Go ahead."

"No, we d—" She reached out and rubbed them anyway, making a noise I'd never heard from her before and then he tapped her hands to move.

"Times up. How about you, little duck?" I ran my nails down his side just light enough to give him goosebumps. "What's wrong, Kent? Balls not blue enough yet?"

"More purple by this point, but I'm gettin' used to it. You can touch a little lower and help me out."

His grin grew, but any response I might have had was interrupted by Stella's suddenly-grating laugh. "Get a room, you two. Unless you're gonna let me watch, of course."

"No room necessary just yet. I'm not done puttin' in the work for a woman like Haddy, but it's okay. I'm a patient man."

"Shame," I teased. "You sound like Ricky."

"Who's Ricky?" Kent asked far too quickly. "For the record, I'd fuck the life out of you right here if you'd let me and you'd forget all about fuckin' Ricky."

My thighs clenched and my hand squeezed the bottle of water I was holding so tightly that the contents sprayed out everywhere. "He's just a friend," I whispered. "Nice guy. Not my type."

To make matters worse, water now dripped down Kent's face and chest, as if he needed any help to look more illegal. "Nice guys don't sound like your type."

Stella reached out again to touch his wet body and when he disappeared into the back once again, she turned to glare at me. "Fuck him for me! Je-sus."

She fanned herself, so I shoved her playfully. "Stop trying to live vicariously through me. He only wants me because I'm the only human he's seen in the last two weeks who hasn't thrown themselves at him. That's *all*. He'll get over it… hopefully."

The falseness of that last word was so obvious that I turned away from her to head back. I didn't need her pointing out that it was a lie and that I looked ready to bend over right there — I already knew that.

Nothing changed the second half of our shift. His accent was making me shiver, his hands on other people made me jealous. He was still as tense as he'd been that morning.

SANTA'SLAY

The end of the day felt like a blessing for both of us, so I ducked into the bathroom to change my clothes and came back out to find Kent with that coat completely off and his pants around his ankles. I didn't know what to focus on first — the tattoos covering every inch of his arms that I hadn't noticed before, the ones covering his legs, or the drool-worthy bulge in his briefs. "I— you—I—"

I panicked and ran into the office, but within seconds, he was on me, pinning me to the wall with nothing on but those briefs. "Where you goin, Haddy? Don't like what you see?"

"Fuck," I hissed, gripping his hips and pulling him closer instead of pushing him away. "Kent!"

"Let me take care of you, little duck." He leaned in so close I was sure he was about to kiss me, but suddenly the door was swinging open and Stella was staring with her eyes popping out of their sockets.

"Fucking hell," Kent whispered sharply and stepped back.

"No no... carry on," she insisted, but the moment had already passed.

"You have shit timing, anyone ever tell you that, Stell?"

"Seriously. For someone that keeps tell-ing me to fuck him, you sure like to stop that from happening." I fixed my clothes with my cheeks burning red and ducked past them both — I needed to get off, and I needed to do it now.

Thank god I didn't live far.

Chapter Six: Santa's Wish

My fingers weren't enough. My vibes weren't enough. I was sweating and frustrated by the time I realized that I needed Kent's cock — craved it like I craved chocolate on a period or tacos on Tuesdays. But craving something I'd never had before was irritating beyond belief, and I was determined to prove to myself that I didn't need him. The duck, the accent, the tattoos, the body, the possessiveness of his touch... I was already catching feelings, which just cemented my original decision.

I couldn't... well, *shouldn't* fuck him.

That didn't mean I couldn't pull out my biggest dildo and pretend for all I was worth, though. I suctioned that thing to the hardwood floor in my bedroom and slid down, more than wet enough to cover it, and whisper-moaned his name as I started to bounce. My nails dug into my thighs as I bounced higher, harder, feeling that silicone head hitting all the right spots. I could only imagine how much better Kent's cock would be, how much harder he'd fuck me, what his voice would sound like whispering filth into my ear. What it would be like to have him tie me down and edge me with that candy cane dildo until I was begging him to let me come.

My thighs burned and my heart was beating too fast for its own good as I pushed myself to keep going, to ride it like I'd ride Kent if I ever had the chance, to rub my clit like it was about to disappear. The fantasies of what could've been if Stella hadn't interrupted played in my mind without filter or shame until I was finally coming, movements erratic and muscles straining, and his was the only name on my lips.

I barely had time to slide off it before my phone rang for the second time since I'd gotten home, so I grumbled under my breath as I grabbed it and flopped back on the bed. "Hello?"

"Hadley! Where the hell have you been?" my sister snapped.

Her voice had never been more unwelcome. "Working. I've been working. Where have you been? Ruin anyone's life lately,

Tia?"

"Just a few. I have a reputation to uphold. Where are you working?"

I rolled my eyes and almost didn't tell her, but I knew her well enough to know she'd figure it out anyway. "CeCe's Toys. I'm a Christmas elf, so go on. Get it out of your system. Make fun of me all you want."

To my surprise, she didn't. "Wait, do you get a discount? I need a new vibe like last year."

"I've got a bunch I haven't even opened yet. You can have one of those; Stella gives them to me all the time." I pulled the sheet over my naked body and stared at the ceiling, wondering if she'd ever get to the point of her call. "Everything okay?"

"Yeah, just bored. Were you busy or something? You sounded out of breath— wait, were you having sex? With who?"

I blushed, peeking over to the 7" pink dildo still standing erect on my floor. "Absolutely not. I was on the treadmill."

"Pfft. Boring. Alright, maybe I'll come see you at work one of these days. You can get back to your damn workout. Your body is perfect by the way. I've always hated you for it."

"Ahh, Tia. Where would I be without your backhanded compliments?" I asked. The truth was, she was every bit as pretty as me, and part of me wanted to keep her away from Kent because of that. "We've been really busy at work, though. Not a lot of time to visit, so maybe you can just come over for dinner or something?"

"Sorry, I fell asleep while you were talking. Come on, it'll be fun. Maybe that bitch will let me be an elf too." She cackled, knowing damn well Stella could hardly stand her. She might hold it together long enough to be professional if Tia showed up, but she would never give her a job.

I didn't know how to answer her without offending her, so I faked a laugh and told her I just didn't think it was a good idea, then hung up to go back to my "workout."

Unfortunately by then, my mood was shot and I cleaned up the mess I'd made with a grimace before climbing right back into bed.

I'd need all the sleep I could get.

~

The next day, I was determined to drive Kent crazy. I'd admitted to myself sometime in the middle of the night that I *had* to fuck him at least once, for my own sanity — and if I was only going to get it once, I needed it to be worth it. So every time he looked at me, I blushed. Every time he came near me, I reached out to touch some part of him. I volunteered quickly to help him put on the festive little bowtie Stella picked out for him, and maybe I let my fingers linger longer than they needed to.

"It looks good on you, Daddy Christmas."

The way he jerked boosted my ego. "You'd look good on me too, y'know?"

"You're right. I would." I ghosted my hand down his chest to his stomach and gasped quietly, knowing it would drive him nuts — and I wasn't disappointed. I could feel him tense, see the way he was contemplating breaking me in half when he finally sank inside of me, and it had me almost desperate for it. "Good thing you're patient, right?"

"Don't know if I am anymore. Patience is becoming overrated. You fuckin' with me, little duck?" He pulled me in by my hip. "'Cause I didn't even make it out of my driveway after having you against that wall."

The thought of him thinking about me and touching himself had me ready to jump into his arms and kiss him right there, but I held steadier than I thought possible. "Should've called me. Would've been more fun to ride you than my dildo."

I pulled away, then turned around and bent over to pick up my purse and move it somewhere else, just for the sake of bending over. When I stood again, he was so hard I could see it through his loose red pants. "Fucking hell," he whispered sharply, trying to adjust himself, and when Stella asked him to sit for customers, he looked pained. "I— I can't, Stell. Tell 'em Santa's feeding the fuckin' reindeer or something."

"Is that—" She looked between us accusingly. "Oh, Santa's got a boner."

Her laugh made him blush for the first time, and I almost felt bad. "Just give him five minutes. They can take their pictures with the slutty elf in the meantime."

"There is a group of dudes out there; I'm sure they'd love that. Come on."

"Dudes? What kinda dudes?" Kent walked over to peek out and scoffed. "Not worried about those cunts." In spite of his words, his erection lowered just a little, but it was still too noticeable for him to walk out there. "How about you let me and Haddy have five minutes back here. She's been so good for Santa, he wants to give her three gifts. Starting with his tongue."

I had just enough decency left inside of my body to tell him "not yet," but that was where it ended. I was done, irrevocably screwed, and I needed to experience him. "Do you have plans after work?"

"Yeah, *you*." His eyes darkened as Stella finally read the room and slipped back to the front. "You're all booked up too, little

45

duck."

My stomach flipped so hard it almost made me nauseous. "Would you look at that. You're right." I flicked my eyes down his frame and finally let myself show how bad I wanted him, then walked — stumbled, really — after Stella, hoping that the rest of the day went much faster than the sex that would follow.

Chapter Seven:
Feeding the Reindeer

The moment the last customer was out, I stared at Stella and jerked my head toward the door. "You can hate me later for this, but I need you to leave. We'll lock up after, I promise."

"Details. I want every single one. Enjoy." She blew me a kiss before leaving, and despite the fact that I knew there were cameras in there, I couldn't find it in me to care.

Kent was still on his throne, his hat tossed to the side and his legs wide open and welcoming. "Would you hate me if I took this jacket off, Haddy?"

"I don't care. I know what you look like both ways, and I promise you can't disappoint me there." I walked forward as he took it off, then straddled his lap and ran my hand through his hair. "Kiss me."

SANTA'SLAY

The growl he released when he slammed our mouths together told me all I needed to know — this was about to be everything I needed. His tongue slid into my mouth possessively, his hands slid under my shirt to touch as much skin as possible, and when he finally pulled them out, he only did so to yank me back by my hair and suck on my neck.

I could feel how huge and hard he was in his pants, and I didn't want to stop even long enough to pull my hose down. "Kent! Oh, fuck... mark me."

I felt his teeth before he sucked my skin in, then heard the fabric ripping between my shaking thighs. He was just as desperate for this as I was, and true to his word, there wasn't an ounce of patience. "Taste so fuckin' good."

Two meaty fingers slid inside of me and he continued marking along my neck as I started to roll my hips. "Kent... I... Do you have a condom? I need more than these fingers."

"Course you do, baby." He pulled out his fingers and sucked them into his mouth, then helped me off so he could shove down his pants. "It's all the way in my truck, but I'm clean and I'll pull out. I lied when I said I had patience. I need you... now."

Red flags shot up everywhere, but the

damned things blended in with the Christmas decor so well that I ignored every single one of them. I climbed back up and lifted my dress to sink down, and the stretch knocked the wind out of me. I buried my face in his neck as he gripped my hips and thrust deeper until he was bottoming out, and I huffed a laugh at the thought that my dildo could ever compare.

"Holy shit, Kent."

"So tight, Haddy. Fuckin' hell. Even better than my imagination." Kent groaned and tipped his head back for me. "Mark me… put it where they'll see."

Some aggressive, possessive part of me woke up in that moment and I need- ed exactly that — needed every customer that walked in here to know I'd marked my territory, that I'd been where they'd only dreamed. I bit, kissed and sucked his skin, giving in fully to the consuming pleasure racing through my body and making me so wet I thought he'd slip out.

He made damn sure he didn't by meeting every bounce with a sharp, hard snap of his hips, and when his thumb found my clit, I leaned back and braced myself on his thighs to give him better access. "God, that feels… please don't stop."

"Wouldn't dream of it. You're so damn beautiful, Hadley. Need you to come all over my cock… been fuckin' dreaming about it."

"Have you?" My breathing picked up as I rode him faster. "Tell me. Tell me what you did to me in those dreams."

"This was one of them, except you feel even better. I ripped your whole costume off and bred you right here on this fuckin' chair." He growled again, fucking up even harder. "Bred you in my truck, against that wall, in my bed with my hand around your throat. Want to fuck you all over this whole town, Haddy."

My first orgasm hit me like a train, making me moan and clench around him as I soaked us both and dug my nails into his skin to stay upright. I needed all of that, needed him everywhere he needed me and then some, and the only word I seemed to know at that point was "Please."

"Say that again." He tugged at the neckline of my dress and sucked my nipple into his mouth, that thumb still working me as his hips sped up.

"Please, Santa," I whimpered. "I— I've been good."

"Ah, fuckin' hell." Kent bit down on my breast and sucked another mark. "Gimme one more, baby. Feel too damn good; you're gonna make me blow."

The pain lanced through me and faded

to pleasure as I leaned back just enough to change the angle. I knew those cameras would see more of me like this — the teeth marks all over my skin, the blush, the sweat, my exposed breasts — and all it did was push me right over the edge again.

My thighs felt like jelly and my whole body was shaking as I dropped forward and let Kent wrap his arms around me and keep me upright. "Do it, Kent," I whispered. "Breed me."

That request alone awoke something inside him, something more primal and animalistic, and he lifted off that chair to fuck up into me. Skin slapped on skin making the wetness sound so obscene I came again, dripping down his cock, and that last orgasm sent him over. He bred me with a growl, his face pressed against my neck, and I tugged his hair as I held him close and tried to catch my breath.

"Are you always that good?" I whispered.

"Yeah, are you?" He huffed a laugh, then kissed my skin again. "Need a fucking cigarette after that and I don't even smoke."

I squirmed, catching him in a proper kiss that I felt down to my toes. "Yes, I'm always that good. I've had a lot of practice."

Kent grinned. "Me too. I like that. Own that shit, little duck." He kissed me again, this time gently and full of more promise

51

than I thought he was capable of. "Come have a drink with me."

For once, I met his eyes without dying inside. "Like together? Right now? I'm down, but… I think I'll need at least twenty minutes before I can walk."

"That's fine with me… unless you mean without my cock inside of you. Then it's not fine."

I could tell he was joking, but he rolled his hips anyway and bit his lip. "You bred me, Santa," I whispered. "Fuck it deeper before we go."

"That's my girl." Kent started moving again, his huge cock still hard enough to stay inside me as I his finger poked at my ass. "Gonna let me have that one day too?"

That single sentence had me throwing out all of my prior reservations. "If it means you're not done with me yet… you can have whatever you want."

Chapter Eight: Bad Santa

Walking into Burning River with Kent was kind of awesome. He looked amazing out of that Santa suit — dark blue henley that made his eyes pop, jeans that made me jealous of denim, and work boots that actually looked like they'd seen work — add in the most enticing cologne I'd ever smelled and a cock that would give me wet dreams for a year, and I was convinced I was walking into that bar with one of the hottest men on the planet.

Heads turned instantly, making me smile a little smugly to myself as I took his arm and let him lead me toward the bar. The bartender, Bane, eyed us both like he thought we were an apparition — and I couldn't blame him; I'd never brought someone into Burning River like that before.

"Where's Stella?" he asked, grabbing two glasses for us as we sat down. "I usually don't see one of you without the other."

I blushed slightly, trying not to think about the time he took us both in his office and let us work off our tabs in a much better way than swiping plastic, then smiled lightly. "She'll be here at some point, I'm sure. I already texted her."

"Hmm." He poured us each two fingers of whiskey and leaned on the bar top. "Who's the new guy?"

"Name's Kent." They shook hands, and I could tell there was some silent man-exchange happening that I would never understand. It wasn't until they let go and Bane introduced himself that the tension hastily slipped away.

"Nice hickeys. Look fresh," Bane joked, making Kent chuckle before taking his first drink.

"Can't believe I drove past this place every day and never noticed it," Kent commented. "Looks like a place with a lot of good memories, eh, Haddy?"

I hummed an agreement and hoped he didn't delve further. "Absolutely. That's why I keep coming back. I've never had a bad time he—"

"Fucking finally!" Stella yelled, rushing over to us. "Tell me all about it, both of you.

Was there penetration? Orgasms? How kinky was it?"

"For fuck's sake, Stell," I laughed. "Just go watch the security tapes."

Her eyes widened so much it was clear she hadn't thought of that prior, and I was pretty sure she considered booking out the doors right then but she glanced at our necks and flicked them. "Beautiful whores."

I licked my lips as I stared at the war zone that had become Kent's neck. I felt a little bad, a little embarrassed, a little juvenile — after all, we were supposed to be grown adults who were out of the hickey stage, but I couldn't deny how good it felt to know my marks were on him and his were on me. They could be covered up with makeup either way. "Something like that."

She sighed dramatically and accepted her drink as Bane handed it to her, then looked right at Kent. "Just give me one detail. Did you Dom her?"

Kent snorted. "The one detail you ask for and it's the one I refuse to tell. I'd never give that answer without consent, but I'll give you somethin' else. Do you still feel my come, Haddy?"

I tilted my head, torn between the instant, thigh-clenching reaction to his question and my confusion at his answer. He hadn't, so why didn't he just say so? Was he just trying to show off, or was this him telling me that if I let him, he wouldn't tell a soul? "I still feel it. I still feel all of you."

Kent polished off his drink with a smirk and got to his feet. "Gonna take a piss."

He slapped my ass before walking off, and Stella tugged on my arm. "He came inside you?"

"No," I lied. "Maybe. I'm on birth control; it's fine. I'll wait a couple weeks and go get Dr. Norelli to give me some penicillin if there's issues. It's fine. I'm fine. Have I said that enough?"

"You have, and every time you said it, I believed you less." Stella huffed and shooed Bane away. "Stop being nosey."

He held his hands up in mock defense and backed away laughing. "Yes, ma'am."

"So will you tell me? Did he Dom you? I swear he does that eyebrow thing just to haunt my dreams. Wait, one more question. Is it as big as we thought?"

"No, he didn't, and no, it's not." I sipped my drink slowly as I watched the disappointment bloom on her face, then smirked. "It's bigger."

"Ugh, I knew it." Stella's eyes locked on something across the bar, and when I turned to see what it was, I saw Kent flirting with another woman. "Dick."

I squirmed in my seat and drank a little heavier. "It's fine. He's probably just being nice to her. Maybe she ambushed him when he came out of the bathroom or something; I don't know. It's not like we're suddenly exclusive."

The defensiveness in my voice made her eyebrows raise in suspicion. "Uh-huh."

"What?" I asked. "I mean it. It's fine." I double-tapped the bar to get Bane's attention as I found myself in need of a refill, but Kent still hadn't come back by the time I needed a third. "Should I go over there?"

"No? Yes. I don't know, but if you do, I'm coming with you." Stella shot back her drink and stood just as Kent finally made his way over. "What was that?" she accused, making Kent frown.

"Nothing. What's your problem?" He waved for another drink, and I found myself wishing I could punch her and disappear at the same time.

"She thought she saw a ghost," I lied. The last thing I needed was for Kent to think I was flipping out over some innocent flirting, especially since I wasn't even sure we were on a date. For a girl like me, that was a cardinal sin. I wasn't supposed to get jealous over flings, especially not if I ever wanted to look them in the eyes again.

"Ah, a ghost." Kent thanked Bane and turned around on his stool looking every bit the wet dream he was, but another woman waved at him and his return grin only pissed me off.

Which… in turn, only made me angrier. I wasn't supposed to care. Wasn't supposed to get upset over something so stupid, and yet, there I was, wanting to rip that girl's face off. "Kent, will you dance with me?" I asked abruptly.

The fact that he looked surprised didn't help matters. "Uh, yeah. I'll dance with you." He finished his drink first, then took my hand and led me to the dance floor, but even as our bodies moved together, his eyes still roamed around the bar.

I gave myself the pep-talk of a lifetime trying not to overreact, yet I couldn't stop myself from trying to steal his attention back. I pressed our bodies a little closer together, leaned up to kiss his chin, and tried the same off-beat dance moves that had Ricky hooked — but Kent struggled to keep up with me. His giant body stumbled, and although I had his attention now, I couldn't tell if he was laughing with me… or *at* me.

"You're strange, little duck." He pulled me back in and kissed my cheek, but that moment was ruined the second another woman strolled over and started dancing behind him.

When he turned to greet her, I swore under my breath and slipped back through the crowd to grab my purse. "Come on, Stell. Let's go find a Santa statue to kick."

Chapter Nine:
Naughty All Year Round

Shaking off that jealous feeling wasn't easy, and I'd barely accomplished it by the time I walked back into work. One look at him had that moving the wrong direction, so I averted my eyes and kept my answers to him clipped.

"Just wasn't feeling the bar scene last night," I lied.

"We were in the middle of dancing. Just don't get why you didn't say somethin'. Left me hanging in the middle of a bar for no damn reason. I had every intention on takin' you home, little duck."

He looked clueless. So clueless it only made me angrier at both of us. "My bad," I said, forcing a fake smile. "I'm sure you fared just fine, though."

"Fared like shite." His accent thickened,

but he reeled it in quickly. "Once I realized you were gone, I went home. I need your damn phone number."

I realized quickly that maybe I'd made a mistake, but it just proved to me I wasn't cut out for this. I loved meaningless sex — loved being able to get what I need and move on, but it took a certain caliber man for something like that. Kent was way, *way* above that caliber, and now I was acting like a spoiled, ridiculous idiot.

"Here." I held out my hand for his phone and then put my number in under 'Little Duck' before passing it back to him. "Now you have it."

He seemed to relax as he smiled down at it, but he instantly hit call to ensure it was mine. When my purse vibrated, he grinned wider. "Good. You can apologize after work."

"Excuse me?" I balked, jaw going slack and hands finding my hips. "I'm not apologizing for anything. If you wanted to hang out with me, you should've hung out with *me.* Not every woman that flashed you a smile."

Kent had the audacity to look shocked. "So I'm not allowed to be friendly? That what you're tellin' me? I wasn't going to fuck any of them. Actually, I was hoping to fuck *you* again, but you fuckin' left. Then the cops came 'cause someone broke their Santa display, and I— whatever. You can apologize after work," he said again, then turned on his heels and went to the front without another word.

I growled in frustration as I followed him.

At least I could take some satisfaction from knowing he knew about the Santa statue. "I'm not apologizing for anything, by the way. I didn't cause a scene or tell you what you could and couldn't do. I just went home. I don't need to apologize for that."

I took my place by the throne as he narrowed his gaze at me, but he kept his mouth shut as the customers spilled in. Regardless of how different he was that day, he still managed to bring in more money than Stella ever had before thanks to the social media posts that blew up. It turned out plenty of women wanted their photo taken with a hot, shirtless Santa.

When break time came around, he was still tense and short, but when he looked at me I could see the smoldering flames behind his eyes. Although I wasn't completely sure what that meant, I couldn't help but be intrigued — and maybe a little turned on, too.

"Still not apologizing," I said cheekily. "You can stop looking at me like that."

"Yeah, we'll see," he quipped, drinking water and then caging me against the wall. "You still have *my* marks all over your neck… you're still mine, little duck."

"You've got my marks too," I retorted, but my voice was shaking and I couldn't stop myself from gripping that red velvet coat. "You have customers, Kent. They're right behind you."

Kent's smirk nearly brought me to my knees. "Fuck the customers," he whispered, then leaned in to kiss me right there in front of everyone.

He broke it as soon as it began, then made his way back to his throne and left me there touching my lips like I'd just been shocked. My legs didn't want to function properly as I took my place again and helped the first woman up the single step and brought her to him.

"Welcome to CeCe's Toys, where everyone's naughty all year round," I mumbled. "Come sit on Santa's lap and tell him what you want."

She winked at me and straddled him, not unlike the way I did. "I think I want Santa," she teased. "How much for a pic with you without the pants?"

Kent closed his eyes and reached out blindly for me. "She's smiling at me, Haddy. Help."

The customer looked taken aback, but

seemed to catch on pretty quickly that she was simply missing a joke.

I blushed and clenched my jaw, then reached over and smacked the top of his head. "Stop it, that's not funny."

He didn't get the memo, because he laughed and went right back to pretending I wasn't there. "So a no-pants picture, eh? No can do, but talk like that will get you on the naughty list."

"It's cute you think I'm not already there," she said, and I was unfortunately unable to stop myself from mocking her under my breath. It was one of those days where the pettiness and cattiness that I normally kept in check was running a little rampant, but what was I supposed to do? I was a woman, and *somebody* was sure as hell gonna hear me roar by the end of the day.

To her credit, she ignored me and got her picture, then blew Kent a kiss on her way out as the next smiley, flirty woman took her place. He waited until she climbed off this time before leaning in. "She smiled at me too. How do I get them to stop?"

"Kent, don't be a dick," I whispered. "You know what the hell I was talking about. We get it, you're annoyingly fucking hot."

"Thank you. That's the nicest thing you've ever said to me." He flashed a tooth- less grin and went back to greeting the next customer, and I did my best to ignore him for the rest of my shift despite all the times he made snarky comments about smiles and girls flirting with him.

The arrogance of that man was unmatched, but as I clocked out and grabbed my clothes to go change in the bathroom, I had to admit that his confidence was at least *mostly* earned. Yes, he was a dick and already had me half ruined, but what if there was a reason for that? What if he was just like me, and that's why he was acting like this?

I pushed open the bathroom door and glared at myself in the mirror as I started to strip. There I was being a fucking idiot again, and no matter how thoroughly I understood that, I couldn't seem to get myself to stop.

"Whatever," I snapped to no one as I tossed the elf costume to the ground. "I'm not apologizing."

The door clicked shut behind me and I turned half-naked to see Kent standing there with a dangerous look in his eyes. "We'll see about that."

Fuck.

Chapter Ten:
Holiday Headspace

"You could've knocked," I grumbled, using my jeans to hide the way he had my thighs clenching with just a phrase. "It's a one-person-at-a-time kind of bathroom."

Him locking the door wasn't a surprise, but the way he reached me in two strides and lifted me onto the sink *was*, especially when he ripped off my panties. "Wet for me already, little duck? You're mad at me... but your pussy isn't."

His fingers slid inside me seconds before he ducked down and flicked his tongue along my clit, and I swore under my breath as my head tipped back against the mirror. "We're all mad at you. You're an ass, Kent."

I felt the vibration of his chuckle through my clit, making me gasp and grind for more without hesitation. It seemed to be the green light he was waiting for to dive in and eat me out like he was determined to kill me, and his tongue was so damned good that I was tempted to let him.

My fingers threaded through his hair and tugged halfheartedly as I remembered I really *was* mad at him, but as his teeth started teasing me and sending little jolts of delicious pain through me, I found myself trying to hold him there. "F-Fuck," I moaned, spreading my legs further as my breathing picked up. "That feels—"

Kent growled as he sucked my swollen clit into his mouth and then started moving those fingers, driving me crazy with ev- ery movement he made. I tried to squirm, tried to argue, tried to convince myself it didn't feel as mind-blowingly amazing as it did — but my body knew better. My thighs clenched around his head and a gasp caught in my throat as I got close, and it only egged him on.

My first orgasm had me nearly scream- ing out in relief so loudly that it echoed off the walls, but he didn't slow in the slight- est. He kept me pinned there, working his tongue as if I didn't just come five seconds ago, and I felt something much more pow- erful building that second time.

"Holy shit," I gasped, digging my nails into his shoulder and trying to keep myself steady on that sink. "Kent, I—" My eyes fluttered closed just as I gave myself over to that mounting pleasure, and there was a moment where I floated out of my body and believed he'd never stop.

I came twice more before I tried to push him back, but he wouldn't budge — and that tongue was making me jerk and twitch with overstimulation so badly that I had tears streaming down my cheeks.

The *best* kind of tears.

His name came out of my mouth as barely more than a whisper, a plea to do something else, *anything* else. To fuck me, choke me, put me on my knees, leave me there like the mess I was, just *something* other than coercing a fifth crashing, messy orgasm from my shocked, sensitive body.

But this was Kent, and Kent wasn't built like that.

He pulled back with a look in his eyes I'd never seen before that kept me frozen in place as his fingers continued to fuck me. "Got somethin' to say, Haddy?"

"What?" I whispered, too foggy and overwhelmed to understand what he was asking. "I … what?"

"You were going to apologize. Not ready yet? Alright, little duck." This time when he leaned in suck my clit, I knew what he was doing, and it dragged a sob from my shaking body.

"I'm—" I wanted to believe I wouldn't say it, but in that moment, I could feel myself slipping into subspace. He owned me, I *wanted* him to own me, and I'd say anything he wanted me to if it meant he wouldn't let me go. "S-Sorry."

I felt him twitch the moment he realized it too, and when he finally started kissing his way back up my body I could see how hard he got just from eating me out. "Taste so fuckin' good, Haddy."

He shoved his pants down and thrust into me before I could respond. I felt myself shattering, sinking, clutching to him like I was drowning, and each rough, desperate thrust that followed had me babbling. "I'm sorry. You're right, I'm — I'm sorry."

"Me too, baby." Our mouths clashed together then, his rough hands lifting me off the sink and spreading my ass so he could fuck harder and deeper. I held on tightly with my arms wrapped around his neck and legs locked behind him, but I knew he wouldn't drop me either way. He had me, totally and completely, and my sixth orgasm proved it.

That had *never* happened to me before.

"Kent…"

"Hadley… I—" He came hard with a growl, biting onto my neck and breathing hard against my skin.

Neither of us moved until we stopped gasping for air, and even then, I didn't move more than I needed to in order to look at him. "I was jealous when I didn't have a right to be, and I took it out on you. You're right. I needed to apologize for that." I kissed him softly, doing my best to ignore the way his smile was growing against my lips.

"And I like the attention women give me too much. I should have kept my focus on you. You deserve that. Do you forgive me? 'Cause if you do, I forgive you too."

I nodded, then placed a single kiss to the corner of his mouth. "Yes, Daddy."

"Daddy," he chuckled darkly. "I prefer Sir, little duck. That stuff at work was just for show." He slid out of me and set me down, reaching back down to play with his come. "What are you doing after work tonight?"

The thought of having to go home alone after what we just did made my breath catch in my throat, so I swallowed quickly. "Nothing. I was just gonna go home."

"You mean *my* home. No bars or loud friends. No other woman's smiles. Just you, in my bed… tied to the headboard."

Kent touched my chin with his pointer finger and I melted, rocking up on my toes with a hopeful expression. "That's exactly what I meant, Sir."

"Good girl." Kent winked and started fixing his clothes, looking much more relaxed than he had all day.

I turned to get dressed and nearly fell over, my legs were so weak — but his strong hands were right there to help me, and all that did was put me deeper into that obedient, beautiful headspace.

Kent *had* me. During sex, after it, it didn't matter. I believed with all of me that I was in good hands, and all I had to do was stop fighting it.

And… maybe stay hydrated enough that I didn't die before he was through with me.

Chapter Eleven: A Little Christmas Bondage

Stepping into Kent's house felt right, and a little more familiar than it should've since I'd never been there before. Maybe it was the smell, or the Christmas decorations that made it seem cozy, or the man himself — but I already loved being there. "Were you serious about tying me to the headboard?" I asked carefully.

"Yes," Kent said simply as he walked over to his fridge and brought me a bottle of water. "After you drink."

"Yes, Sir." I smirked playfully as I took a sip, then pushed him onto the couch and straddled his lap. "I need a little break unless you want to listen to me cry the next time you make me come."

Kent chuckled, his hand finding a home on my hips as he watched me drink more. "Won't make you cry, little duck. But we can take a break and I'll order us some dinner. Any particular craving besides my cock?"

"Tacos, maybe? That seems like a terrible idea, though... especially if you want my ass, too." I kissed him quickly and took another sip. "Maybe I'll just eat when you let me go."

Kent grinned, seemingly getting an idea from that, and he pointed at my water while he grabbed his phone to order food. When we both finished, he bit his lip and slid his hand up my thigh. "You ever cockwarm for someone before, gorgeous?"

"No. I know what it is... just never had someone that could sit still with their cock inside my body." I leaned in to flick my tongue over his ear and whispered, "Which hole, Sir?"

"Fucking hell." He thumbed my lip with his finger and tugged me forward. "This one, baby girl."

My stomach went somewhere other than where it should be in a violent and obnoxious manner — like an American — and I nodded breathlessly. "Yes, Sir."

I rolled my hips to make sure he was nice and hard, then kissed him until his food arrived and he tossed me off his lap like I was a doll. Knowing how strong he really was only made me more eager to please him, so I followed him into the kitchen and kneeled under the table to wait.

"Who knew you were such a good girl… or are you just my good girl now?" Kent pulled out his cock and sat down, spreading his legs wide for me to perfectly fit between them.

"I've always been a good girl, Sir. But now it's just for you." I kissed and licked up his shaft before sucking him in and humming happily, then worked his cock deeper until I could rest my cheek against his thigh and hold him there.

He seemed to take his time staring at me before he finally leaned forward and ate his meal. "Wanted you just like this the moment I saw you. Never seen someone so beautiful in my life."

It was hard not to believe him. I sucked gently as an unspoken "thank you" and let my eyes close, just enjoying the way he felt stretching my throat. Enjoying the way he smelled, even down there.

When he finished eating, his heavy hand patted my head softly. "Up, little duck. It's time for Santa to play with the most beautiful elf he's ever seen."

I forced my eyes open again and sucked as I slid off, then wiped my mouth with the back of my hand as I stood on shaky legs. "I could've fallen asleep like that."

"One day, you will." Kent carried me to the bedroom, once again tossing me with ease then walking back out of the room. When he came back this time, he had Christmas lights in his hands, and I realized he had no intentions on using rope for this. "How many limbs do you consent to?"

I studied him, the huge, comfort- able-looking bed, and then the lights that he brought and took a deep, steadying breath. "All of them, Sir. I trust you. Just… please don't leave the room with me tied like that. Just this first time."

"Of course, baby girl." He took so long restraining me that it felt like torture, but even after he finished, he didn't stop touch-ing me. His fingers ghosted over my skin and left goosebumps in their wake, then he reached into his back pocket and pulled out one of the last things I'd expected to see — a skinny Christmas tree branch. "It's one of the softer ones. I really want to see your skin bounce under its touch. That okay, Hadley?"

"Yes, Sir." I squirmed just to test the lights, and I was pleased when I could bare-ly move at all. "You can do whatever you want."

"That's my girl. Such a good girl for me.

Know how hard you make me when you call me that?"

The first touch of fir had me twitching and trying to look at my belly button.

"Breathe for me, Haddy. I'm gonna take care of you."

The praise and the attention were overwhelming from a man like that. I shivered and slowly relaxed, gasping quietly as he dragged the tip of that branch down the inside of my thigh. "That feels good."

"Yeah?" He slid it over to my clit. "Still?" I shivered and nodded quickly. "Yes, Sir." I was no stranger to using unconventional toys — I'd gotten myself off one time with the round part of a spoon once just to prove I could — but I'd never felt anything quite like that before, conventional or not. It was prickly yet soft like he'd said, and each of the needles felt like tiny little fingers caressing and teasing my skin.

"Look at my good girl. You really are gorgeous, little duck." Kent leaned in and kissed along my breast, spending extra time on my small birthmark and then grinning up at me. "Every inch of you."

"So are you." I curled my fingers around the warm, lit lights and tried to keep my breathing steady as I waited for him to make his next move. "I'm all yours, Sir."

It brought a genuine smile to his face,

one that made me return it without even re-
alizing. "For the record, out of all the wom-
en's smiles out there, yours is the best."

Thick digits slid back inside me and stole
the breath from my lungs, but I wasn't
missing it. "Sir… please." I rolled my hips as
much as I could and chased more of him. "I
need you."

"Tell me what you need exactly, baby
girl." He hooked his fingers and rubbed my
clit with his thumb, making me whimper and
strain from overstimulation.

I could barely think straight enough to
answer him, but the more he applied that
beautiful, painful pressure, the more desperate I was to have him inside of me.
"Fuck me, Sir. I don't care what hole."

Kent met my gaze and explained what
he was going to do before he did it. He
wanted my ass, and in order to do so, he
was going to untie me and retie me once I
was on my belly. It took about five minutes
since Kent was extra careful during the pro-
cess, but I couldn't complain.

When I was restrained, he started with
some lube, warming it and pressing it
against my tight hole. "You ever been
fucked in the ass, Haddy?"

"Yes, Sir. I have. A few times."

Kent slid his finger in with a groan, rubbing my back with his left hand to relax me.

"How about by a cock this size?"

I smirked as I buried my face in his pillow and shook my head. "No, Sir. Bet you're gonna fill me up so good."

"Damn right, I am." His palm slapped down on my ass, and after he squeezed my cheek, I felt his finger work me open more. I tried not to clench too much as his movements got quicker, rougher, less patient — but everything he did felt amazing and I was riding a high I'd almost forgotten existed.

By the time he leaned down to bite my ass and pull his fingers out, I was a moaning, sweaty, writhing mess. The lights weren't hot, but they were warm enough that they were fucking with my internal temperature in the best way and making me ache for him.

"Sir, please," I moaned.

"Want my cock, don't you, baby? I got you."

I felt the bed dip under his weight as his heavy length slid up the back of my leg just to torture me. Pleas fell from my lips like snow on the ground outside, but the bastard wasn't done messing with me just yet — the broad, smooth head of his cock stretched me open and left me entirely not once, not twice... *five* times before he finally sank fully inside of me. By then, I was biting the sheet to stop myself from outright begging, but his body pressing me into the mattress was grounding me.

Still, he kissed all along my back and shoulders, rolling his hips every few seconds just to make me squirm. "So tight, Haddy. Breathe."

"Yes, Sir." I slowly uncurled my fingers and relaxed my tense muscles, letting each of his whispered praises help me breathe easier. "I'm okay."

"Good. Now let me change that." Even without seeing him, I knew he had a huge grin on his face as he sat up and gripped my hips, but before I could ask him to elaborate, he pulled out and slammed back in.

I yelped as I felt it in every ruined, hooked inch of my body. Blood, lust, fear, and pleasure all raced under my skin until the second sharp thrust stopped them all in their tracks and made me choke on the moan that forced its way out. "S-Si—"

Kent's palm gripped the back of my neck, shoving me into that pillow as he took my ass completely apart, and I lost all perception of anything that wasn't him after that.

Though I felt like one of those sex toys Stella was always throwing my way, an orgasm was building in my gut and I couldn't deny how much it turned me on. "Don't stop," I whispered, arching my back and tugging hard on those lights a second before I started to squirt all over him and his flannel sheets.

It was all I had left. I was drained, strung out, shaking so violently when he bred my wrecked little ass that it was a miracle he was holding me still enough to finish the job, and I barely registered him calling my name and kissing over my skin as he untied me.

I was good — better than good — I just… couldn't find the words to tell him that yet.

Chapter Twelve:
Caroling on the Couch

The next two hours were a blur. I vaguely remembered him carrying me to the bath, cleaning me up, and feeding me those tacos I ordered that had long since gone soggy, but I didn't really feel awake again until I had a bottle of water in my system and a mug of hot chocolate in my hand. The whole time, I'd managed to ignore his looks of concern and the intensity behind his eyes, though it was a lot harder to pull that off now that we were entwined together on the couch by the fireplace.

"I'm fine, Sir. I promise. I mean… my ass is sore, my clit is still throbbing, and my limbs all feel like molten lava, but I love it. It's just a reminder of how good you were to me." Saying that to *him* of all people felt strange, but I couldn't deny the accuracy of those words. "So thank you."

"You're welcome," he said with a chaste kiss. "And thank you for being so good for me. Everyone before you was just a disappointment. I didn't mean to push you too hard but I had to be sure. Now I know."

I also ignored the blush tinting my cheeks as I braced myself for where this conversation would head. "So, now that your curiosity is satisfied, what next?"

"Don't think I'll ever stop being curious, but what's next is more of this. At least for tonight, I don't want to make you even more sore."

It was too ambiguous for me to make out whether or not he even understood the question, but I was tired and feeling unusually… needy. There was no other word for it. I almost always felt like this after subbing for someone, especially someone new, but something about this felt different. Like the usual afterglow had been kicked up high enough to light up a high school football stadium.

"I appreciate that, but for any record that matters… I like it. I don't necessarily want to be in pain, but I like feeling it for a couple of days. It reminds me I did better than the time before, if that makes any sense. Kind of like a workout. Your muscles don't get sore when you stop pushing yourself to be better."

"And you've got a beautiful mind to match your beautiful… everything else." Kent kissed my nose and pulled me in even clos- er. "I'm from Cornwall by the way. England. I just moved here when I was ten so my accent is fairly faint… or I thought it was before you pointed it out."

I chuckled and melted into his arms, determined to soak as much of this up as I could before he turned back into the cocky, infuriating man I knew him to be. "I've always had a good ear for accents. Surprised I didn't guess that."

"Probably too distracted with how badly you wanted to fuck me. I forgive you." Some of his cockiness may have surfaced there, but the energy around us remained unchanged. "How old are you, Haddy?"

"I'll be thirty in March. How old are you? I might be good with accents, but I'm awful at aging people. I feel like you could either be twenty-five or forty," I teased. "Is that why you prefer Sir to Daddy? Because the last one could be true?"

"Guess I'm bad at it, too. Thought you were twenty-four at best. I'm thirty-three."

I grinned cheekily. "Disappointed you're not robbing cradles here?"

"Nah, you're still my baby girl." Kent chuckled. "You got any family close by? Did you mention a sister, or was that Stella?"

"It was me, probably. Her name is Tia, but you're never allowed to meet her," I said quickly. "Ever."

He seemed to think that was hilarious. "Why not?"

"Because I'm a dumpster fire of a person and I seem to overreact when it comes to you, and I *know* I overreact when it comes to her. See? I'm being a mature human being and admitting my flaws, so you can't be mad at me for it, Sir." I reached over and slid my hand up his thigh to distract him further. "Do we have to talk about her? What about you? Any siblings?"

"A brother. And I don't wanna talk about him while you touch me there either." The music shifted as he leaned in for a proper kiss, and when "Santa Baby" came on, he smirked against my lips. "You should sing this to me."

Instead, he started belting it out, and his voice was so high I was sure he couldn't go higher if he tried. It was like nails on a chalkboard, and I smacked his arm with a loud laugh when he started changing the lyrics.

"Kent, you're ridiculous. You're a ridiculous human being."

"Yeah, I am, but what's that say about you, little duck?"

The smile on my face faded. "Probably nothing good, honestly, but it's fine. We can be ridiculous together." I flipped to straddle him and lightly touched his cheek, brushing my thumb over the stubble just above his beard as I tried to memorize the look in his eyes. "Are you tired yet?"

"As much as I want to say something cheesy like 'I've never felt more alive,' I'm fuckin' beat, Haddy. Could probably squeeze in a Christmas movie before I knock out though."

I kissed him gently and bit his lip as I pulled back so we could lay down. "You're really into the holidays, huh? It's just a Daddy Christmas thing?"

"Yeah, it's my favorite time of year. Never imagined I'd be able to dress up like Santa until I had kids or something, though. Glad I was wrong." Kent stretched enough to make his back pop and then wrapped his arms around me, and I found myself won- dering what kind of Santa he'd be if he was allowed to have the full outfit instead of the sexy one.

I had a million questions for him, from whether or not he tied people up with Christmas lights often to how many kids he wanted, but the contrast there only served to remind me how in over my head I was. His hands were ghosting down my body and making me horny, the sudden shift in the way he was treating me had me confused, and when the intro to *The Holiday* started, I worried I was a little bit in love.

"So how far does your Santa obses- sion go?" I asked teasingly, determined to change the subject before I asked him to marry me. "Do you want to come down my chimney and give me presents?"

"Hell yeah, I do. I mean, I don't imagine I'd fit in the chimney, but I guess my ob- session does go a little deeper than I've let on. I'd love to come in your house while you're sleeping and give you a present. But only if you had cookies for me after."

My thighs clenched so hard that I knew "horny" was winning out of those three emotions. "You mean like… sneak in and take me? Or do you actually mean come in the front door, leave gifts under the tree and steal my chocolate chip cookies?"

"Well, I think you have to give me a key so you can find out. But if it *was* the former, are you opposed?"

The simultaneous rush of adrenaline through my chest and wetness between my legs answered the question before I could string the words together in my mind, but that seemed like something I wouldn't want to do with someone that wasn't my actual Dom. For the first time, I had to confront the fact that I *wanted* him to be my Dom — for a lot longer than the length of a fling — but I wasn't sure I was ready to admit that out loud yet.

"Maybe," I said simply. "Maybe not. Guess you'll find out if I ever hand you a key."

Chapter Thirteen: Christmas Cat Fight

Every inch of my body was sore as I stuffed myself into that little elf costume the next day. I could feel the memory of his thick, brutal cock with each step I took, and the vibrating plug he'd pushed into my wrecked ass wasn't helping in the slightest.

It was also ensuring that I was almost permanently wet, which proved to be way worse than it sounded when I stepped out into the frigid December air and barely had any fabric at all protecting my pussy from the wind. Even Kent's leather jacket wasn't helping much, though the scent of his cologne and the feeling of his hand on my lower back was doing *something* for me.

"How long do I have to keep this in?" I whispered as we ducked inside CeCe's Toys.

"Until I get to fuck you in the bathroom again." Kent leaned in to kiss my cheek, then trailed across to my lips, not caring in the slightest who was watching.

I grinned, fisting my hands in the fuzzy part of his Santa coat. "Make it the office this time. I want the video."

His sneer sent a chill up my spine. "Good girl." Kent bit my cheek hard enough to make me twitch and walked away to his throne.

Something about him up there looked different. I couldn't tell if it was my marks along his neck and bare chest or how he looked even more confident than ever before, but either way, it took all of my self-control not to ride him right there in front of everyone.

Especially when I saw the change in the way he was treating the customers. Sure, he was still flirty and handsy, but the look in his eyes was different. He was playing a role now, nothing more, and that had me re-laxing and joining in right up until my sister paid us a visit.

Her jaw dropped as she took in Kent's gorgeous body, and she wasted no time at all striding over, pushing her way to the front of the line, and climbing into his lap like she owned him. "I don't know about the rest of them, but I'm *absolutely* on the naughty list, Santa."

"O-Okay…" Kent chuckled a little awkwardly. "And what's Santa supposed to do about that since you seem to have all the answers?"

I didn't hear her response after she uttered the words "punish me." The idea that Kent would touch her, that she thought this was a good idea somehow, that she came here after I expressly told her not to — I grabbed Tia by her perfect ponytail and yanked her off of his lap without hesitation.

"Can you keep it in your pants for five seconds?" I hissed, letting her stand once we were both off the platform. "He's not for you."

Stella settled the rest of the patrons as Kent steered us toward the back. "Damn, little duck. It's okay. Wasn't actually gonna do it."

"You weren't?" Tia scoffed. "Whatever. What the *hell*, Hadley! That was embarrassing!" She fixed her hair and glared at me. "Didn't know he was claimed."

Kent put an arm around me to help me calm down. "Didn't see the many claim- ing marks I have on me? Pretty sure she spelled her name out at some point."

My neck wasn't any better, but I opted not to point it out in that moment. "I asked you not to come here, Tia. You never listen to me."

"I shouldn't have to listen to you. I'm a grown woman, and judging by what just happened, I can't say the same for you." She turned her attention to Kent as my stomach sank. "That's what does it for you, huh? Insecure little girls?"

All amusement faded from Kent's face. "Don't know what you're insinuating, but you don't know shit about anything. You cut in front of the line like a little girl, pouted like a little girl, and now you're trying to embarrass your only sister like a little girl. And nothing about you is my type. I can see why you don't talk about her much, Haddy. Not much to say." He kissed my cheek and went back to the front, leaving Tia with her jaw slack and staring at the door.

I grinned like the child she was making me out to be. "Have a good day, Sis. Thanks for stopping by."

Tia scoffed as she stormed out, and within seconds, Stella was rushing over to me. "I still hate her, but seeing you snatch her up by her hair was gold. One of the customers got a photo. Want to see it? They already sent it to me."

"I'd rather pretend that never happened. I need a couple of minutes, though… for personal reasons." I grimaced as I walked stiffly toward the bathroom — at some point during that scuffle, my plug had shifted, but I barely had time to get it fixed before the damned thing started vibrating inside of me. "Kent!" I gasped, spinning around and expecting to see him.

When I didn't, I waited a full three minutes before accepting the fact that he was doing this to fuck with me and walked back out to join him. The Christmas music was loud enough to drown out the vibrations, but I couldn't stand still — and Kent had the audacity to have the tiny remote right there on the armrest where anyone could see it.

When a woman sat on his lap, I watched him press through the settings. He smiled and listened to her like there was absolutely nothing else going on, but all I could see was his fat thumb pressing that damned button over and over with a grin I suddenly wanted to slap.

One particular setting had me gasping audibly and reaching over to grip the back of his throne. It was making my legs shake, making me so wet I could feel it, and the bastard ignored my presence beyond that stupid remote.

By the time break rolled around, I was snatching *him* off that throne and drag- ging him to the back office. When the door closed behind us, he lifted me off the floor and pressed me against it, smiling with a dangerous glint in his eyes. "What's wrong, little duck?"

I twitched as that plug continued to vibrate. My hair was matted to my forehead from the near hour-long torture I'd just endured and every inch of me was trembling with need, but I wasn't quite deep enough in subspace to beg for it yet. "Just didn't want to waste time, Sir."

"I can see that." Kent slipped his hand under my dress and into my tights, toying with the vibrator as he kissed me deeply.

The possession in that kiss had me slipping fully into the right headspace. I sucked his tongue as I rolled my hips, needing more contact, more of him. "Sir…"

He set me down and stripped me naked, but instead of pulling down his own pants like I expected, he reached into his pocket to retrieve a clear bag with one of Stella's candy cane dildos inside of it. "I cleaned it, promise. I know I've been torturing you today, baby, but I'm not done yet."

I shuddered, tipping my head back against the door and nodding. "I trust you, Sir. Will you let me come?"

"Of course. Love it when you come. Just once for now though, sweetheart. The rest of them belong to me and only me." I gasped as that thick dildo slid inside me, adding extra pressure to the plug still inside my ass, but I grinned when even that couldn't compare to Kent's cock.

I was sure he picked a size smaller than him on purpose. It was just enough to have me spreading my legs further and trying to rock down on it, but not enough to really send me over — until he pulled it out and tossed me onto Stella's desk and I realized that camera was pointing directly at my splayed legs, stuffed ass and dripping, desperate pussy. "Oh, fu—" My hands found the back of her desk as I laid almost all the way back, letting him slide the dildo back into me. "Please," I whispered.

"Please what, Hadley?" He kept his pace excruciatingly slow. "Harder? Slower? You want to come all over your friend's desk?"

My eyes fluttered closed as I started trying to fuck myself on it. "Yes, Sir."

Kent's movements stopped altogether. "Yes, what?" he growled, his body tensing right before my eyes.

My thighs clenched at the look he was giving me. "Harder, Sir," I whispered, biting my bottom lip and glancing up through my lashes to meet his eyes. "I want to come all over Stella's desk."

"Good girl. Come for me." Kent leaned down and sucked my clit into his mouth, fucking into me perfectly with that silicone Christmas cock, and the three intense sensations had me not just coming, but squirting all over his face and last month's AR reports.

It felt so good that I didn't care if Stella wanted to kill me or not. But I needed the real thing, and I needed it an hour ago. "Sir, please! Need you," I moaned. "Show her how well you fuck me. Show them all."

Kent wiped off his beard and shoved his velvet pants down, his giant cock springing free as he tossed the fake one aside and thrust inside of me. "Fucking hell, I need you."

Our lips crashed together, and he wasted no time fucking me so hard the desk groaned under us. I screamed his name as each rough snap of his hips shifted the plug inside of me, and he dragged another orgasm out of my breathless, pliant body almost instantly.

My nails raked down his bare, muscular back as he filled me up with a growl, humping into me after like he needed his come as deep as possible, and when he finally stilled, he didn't pull out of me.

We were late as hell coming back from that break, but I didn't care, and it was obvious he didn't, either. We were right where we needed to be.

Chapter Fourteen:
Sleigh Ride

Much to my surprise, I received a text from Kent on Friday night that said "be ready in ten." Luckily, I'd showered that morning, but I couldn't help but wonder what he wanted — just another night of the best sex I'd ever had, or were we finally going to go on an actual date?

In anticipation of the latter, I put on one of my favorite red dresses and a pair of boots to keep me warm, then grabbed my purse with a little surprise in it just in time for him to knock on my door. I opened it quickly and stepped out onto my porch with flushed cheeks and a soft smile on my face, but my jaw dropped when I looked past Kent to see his... vehicle.

It wasn't a car, or a truck, or a van, or even a motorcycle. No, Kent Baker had shown up to my house in a horse-drawn carriage, and I found myself rooted to the spot. "What is that?" I asked dumbly.

"Santa's ride. What'd you expect? I couldn't afford reindeer," he joked, leaning in to kiss my cheek. "You look beautiful. I got a blanket for us in the sleigh."

Was it possible to fall in love in a month? Maybe, maybe not, but in that moment, no one could've convinced me that I wasn't in love with him. "Are you serious? This is serious? You did this?" I took his hand and led him forward excitedly, offering a quick greeting to the coachman before climbing in. "This is insane."

"Insane, ridiculous... you've almost figured out all my middle names." Kent climbed in and placed a red blanket over our laps, then pulled me in as the carriage began to move.

I huffed a surprised, floored laugh. "What are the rest of them?"

"Don't know yet, you weren't supposed to ask." Kent joined in and tugged my hair slightly. "Have a feelin' you'll figure them out one day."

"One day, huh?" I leaned a little closer. "Plan on keeping me around then, Santa?"

Those gorgeous blue eyes locked with mine, and when he kissed me without saying a word, I felt the answer deep in my bones. "Would that be a bad thing, little duck?"

"No, Sir." I'd planned on waiting until later to give him the surprise I'd brought, but now, it had more than one meaning. I reached into my purse and fished out the small, silver key, then handed it to him as the nervousness in my chest mounted. "Take this."

His hand wrapped around mine and tugged me in closely again. "This mean what I think it means? 'Cause you been a good girl, Haddy. Such a good girl for me."

My stomach flipped. "Yes, Sir."

He pocketed the key and slid his hand under the blanket, ghosting his fingertips along my thigh as they slid up my dress. "Open."

I didn't bother glancing toward the coach-man as I spread my legs willingly for him to let him in. The blanket would hide me, and even if it didn't, he wasn't facing us — and I certainly didn't have the strength to tell Kent to stop as he kissed down my neck and slipped his fingers inside my body. It was crazy to me how good they felt, how much better they were than most cocks I'd experienced, and when I felt him harden against my leg, I gasped.

"Shhh," he whispered. "Need to see how long you can stay quiet for me."

The contrast of his blazingly warm hand against the freezing night air had me breathless anyway — speechless, soundless, all the things he wanted me to be as those horses carried us through the streets and he brought me closer to orgasm. I squirmed, needing more, needing him to forgo public decency and take me right there, but he kept his movements steady and sure in spite of how tightly his other hand was squeezing me.

"So beautiful like this, Hadley. Tell me only I get to see you this way."

He kept his voice low, just for me, and I knew it was only fair to return the favor. "Only you, Sir. No one else."

"Good girl… I want to fuck you right here so badly, baby girl. Come for me." His teeth latched onto my neck, but I needed to give him more than that.

The street was empty anyway, so I shook my head quickly and pushed his hand away, then flipped to straddle him and pulled the blanket up around our shoulders so no one could see us. "It's cold, Santa. Let me keep you… warm."

I couldn't see what he was doing, but I knew he was pulling out his cock and positioning so he could slide inside me. We moaned together as he inched his way in, and when he was bottomed out, he lifted my dress above my ass so he could rest his hands there. "Nice and warm now, baby."

"Me too." I kissed him deeply, ignoring the spikes of panic and fear at the fact that we were doing what we were doing, and simply enjoying how it felt to give in. I had no idea where he was taking me — and therefore no idea how much time we had before we'd arrive — so I didn't bother holding back as I started to move. "Feels so good, Sir."

"You always do." Nails raked my thighs as I bounced, and his mouth became more insistent by the second as he nibbled along my breasts, making me wish I was naked for him, even here.

I caught myself moaning and clamped my jaw shut, then tried to keep myself quiet as I came all over his cock. I heard him growl a split second before he began barreling up into me, and when he took over, there was no finesse, no hiding what we were doing as the blanket slipped down my back.

But Kent didn't care in the slightest. He stared at me with lust-blown eyes, fucking me as if we were the only people in the vicinity, and when he came deep inside me, he groaned my name so loud I heard the echo through the snowy street.

It was… altering.

I kissed him hopelessly, madly, shaking with need and the freezing night air, but his arms never left me.

Not for a moment.

"Kent," I whispered, psyching myself up to ask the question I was most afraid to. "Sir... am I the only one who gets *you* like this?"

He nodded, still breathing hard when he finally met my gaze again. "Course you are. Haven't wanted anyone else since I laid eyes on you, little duck."

The coachman cleared his throat. "You asked for a warning earlier, Sir. Next street's going to have more people than here."

For a moment, Kent didn't seem like he'd let me go at all, but when he pulled me off of his lap and handed me a napkin, I hastily cleaned up and got back under his blanket.

"You sounded a little worried there, Haddy. I meant what I said. There's been no one else."

I studied the city around us with the decorated street lamps, colorful lights adoring the storefronts, and the magic of the sleigh we were in, then took a deep breath. "I'm not good at this, Kent," I said gently. "I'm sure you've seen that by now... but I want to be. I don't want this to just be a fling."

"Good thing I'm great at this, eh?" he

joked, kissing along my face playfully. "We'll figure it out together. You're mine now. No goin' back."

Every part of me knew he meant it, and suddenly, I didn't care where that carriage was headed.

I'd have gone anywhere with him.

Chapter Fifteen:
Silent Night

Several days passed without Kent mentioning the key or using it for what we'd discussed. Every night, I went to bed in a loose t-shirt and panties hoping he'd show up and take me — but it never happened, and somehow, Christmas Eve had already rolled around.

I had no desire to see Tia and we had no other living relatives, so after a brief hour at Burning River with Stella and Bane, I curled up on my couch in my fuzzy reindeer socks and started my yearly tradition of watching every *Psych* Christmas episode back-to-back. The mug of hot chocolate warmed my fingers as I watched and wondered where Kent was, what his Christmas Eve looked like. I imagined he'd be somewhere with family or friends, dressing up as a slightly more appropriate Santa since that *was* his day after all, but that singular thought reminded me of something very important.

Kent was Santa.

Santa came down the chimneys of strangers on Christmas Eve to deliver presents.

It was Christmas Eve.

If I had to take everything I knew about Kent and make an educated guess, I'd have said he hadn't used the key yet because he was waiting for that night. It was cheesy, ridiculous, and maybe a little stupid, but the thought of engaging in *that* kind of play on Christmas Eve with someone dressed like Santa had every "so wrong, it's hot" cylinder firing inside of me.

For the first time in twenty years, I felt how people were supposed to feel the night before Christmas. It was just for an extremely dirty, one-way-ticket-to-Hell kind of reason, and I couldn't have been more here for it.

I raced to my bathroom to spot check the half-assed shaving job I'd done, then brushed my teeth before climbing into bed with my heart pounding and my pussy so wet that it was a struggle not to touch myself. But Kent had made it clear that my orgasms belonged to him, and I was a good girl. I wouldn't come until he was roughly pinning me to this very bed and taking me like I was a plate of cookies left out for him.

The thought made me laugh, but there was nothing funny about it, particularly when another hour passed without any sign of him. I considered sending him a text to see what he was doing, but I didn't want to know — if he said he was busy, I'd be disappointed, and I didn't want to have a warning if he was really on his way.

I *wanted* the fear.

Unfortunately, that meant I laid there so long in silence that I fell asleep, and not even the sound of the front door closing woke me up. I didn't stir at all until I felt his rough hand sliding up my thigh, and the second my eyes opened, his other one clamped over my mouth.

"Shhh. Supposed to be a silent night, baby girl." He only moved it away to rip the clothes from my body, and when he climbed on my bed fully dressed, I felt a chill travel up my spine. He smelled like my favorite cologne and the very cookies I left out for him as he slotted between my legs and started pulling out his cock, and I struggled to keep quiet as I splayed myself open for him.

"Good girl," he whispered, but he slid three fat fingers inside of me instead of his hard, throbbing length. "Already so wet for me."

How could I not be? I rocked my hips and decided to test him — to see how far this fantasy really went for both of us. I looped my legs over his shoulders and pushed him back, then scrambled toward the edge of the bed.

The growl he released had me crav- ing the manhandling that I was sure was coming, and he didn't disappoint. I almost yelped as he slammed me back into the position he wanted me in, this time on my belly. "Naughty little duck."

He pinned me there and spanked my ass, making me clench and squirm under him, but I was stuck. I couldn't get out even if I wanted to, and the truth of that had me wet and shaking. *Come on, Kent,* I urged silently. *Take me.*

After two more quick, sharp smacks, I felt him drop down and line himself up. He eased his way in so painfully slowly I nearly yelled at him, but the second he bottomed out, that hand returned to my mouth to stop me from making a sound.

Fuck. I squeezed my eyes shut as he forced himself so deep it made my back arch, and then he just fucking took it. He fucked me without any regard for me. He fucked me for the power, for *his* pleasure only, and something about that was so hot it had me coming a few minutes in and whimpering into his hand.

True to form, he didn't let up. He had no intentions of letting up until I was a sore, pliant mess, and when his nails dug into my skin, it nearly sent me over again. "Santa's little sex toy. Gonna fucking ruin you, slutty little elf."

I couldn't stay silent. I moaned, louder with each thrust, gripping the sheets and clenching around him until he shoved my face further into the pillow. Breathing became difficult as he drilled into me, and just as I began to float, he pinned us together and flooded my pussy with a long, drawn-out groan.

His body weight was heavy enough on top of me that I still couldn't move. I stayed there, stuffed full of his pulsing cock, limbs trembling and face smothered until he had to let me up for air. My heart raced as I gasped, filling my lungs again and again as he fucked his come a little deeper. "Sir—"

Kent tugged my head back by my hair and kissed along my face, grinding slow and deep. "You're mine, Hadley. Only mine."

I'd never been one to get off from slow and steady sex before. I needed it fast, rough, hitting all the right spots — but this? Those words, those steady, sure movements… I felt another orgasm building in my gut. "Yours, Sir. Can I clean your cock?"

He stilled, nipping my cheek to show how pleased he was before he pulled out. "Fuckin' perfect."

Kent flipped me over again and finally stripped before straddling my chest, and I licked the head just to tease him as I wiggled my arm under his thigh down between my own legs. "Can I touch myself while I do it, Sir?"

"Course you can. Been a good girl for me. Gonna come while you choke on Santa's cock?"

Before I could answer, he slapped my lips with it and made me shudder. "Yes, Sir. Or should I call you Santa tonight?"

I sucked him in without waiting, moaning softly at the taste of my own pussy as I rubbed my clit and bobbed my head off the mattress to take him deeper. His fin- gers threaded through my hair and helped me, urging me faster, making me take more, and I came as he slid all the way into my throat just like he wanted me to. He groaned, praising me over and over until he was spilling into my throat with more come than I expected, especially since I hadn't been expecting it at all.

He pulled out to let me swallow and then shoved it right back in to make me cockwarm while he caught his breath. I played with his balls and kept my eyes on his gorgeous face until he was ready to move, then sat up and grinned sleepily as I felt the mess dripping out of me. "I think we need to do this more often, Sir."

"We will. You're not gettin' this key back." He collapsed on the bed next to me and pulled me to his chest. "Missed you today."

I grinned, leaning up to kiss his cheek. "I missed you too. Do you have time for me tomorrow, or should I give you your present now?"

"'Course I have time for you." Kent's fingers found my hair, and the soft, gentle touches made me melt. "We should get cleaned up and sleep, little duck. I'm not going anywhere."

And in that moment, I realized that I wasn't either.

Chapter Sixteen:
Someday at Christmas

Christmas morning, I cockwarmed for Kent during breakfast and then rode him on the kitchen floor. We showered together, never getting more than two feet apart as we got dressed and ready to leave, and I couldn't believe how attached I was to him. It wasn't just the sex, either. I held his hand as he drove us to his house, laughed as he sang along to carols on the radio, and swooned when he opened my door after parking.

I was hooked on *all* of him.

"Is this where you wanted me to close my eyes?" I asked.

"Yeah. Do you trust me?" His blue eyes bore into mine, still making me as weak as they had that first day.

"Yes, Sir. Of course I do."

He lifted me off the ground the second I closed them, and although he struggled a little with unlocking his door, he managed to get me inside without bonking my head on anything. "Alright, baby. You can look."

His house was filled with ducks of all kinds. Most were stuffed, some were bath toys, some were even ceramic and looked hand-painted. I was overwhelmed and speechless, clinging to him as I kissed all over his face for thinking of me like that. "You're incredible, Sir. They're amazing."

He blushed, closing his door behind me and ushering me inside. "First, you really need to tell me more about things you like or find cute, or you'll just end up with fifty more ducks in the near future. Second, your real gift is hidden under one of these duck's bums. You got to find it."

"Seriously?" I giggled, wiggling out of his arms and starting the search for my oth- er present. I didn't care what he said, the ducks were real gifts too, but curiosity was overtaking me as I lifted up feathered ass after feathered ass and found nothing.

I must've checked thirty before I finally found it.

It was wrapped like a five-year-old had done it, and somehow I knew it was just how Kent wrapped presents. I tore it open, gasping when the small box fell to the floor out of my shaking hands, and I opened it carefully to find a gorgeous necklace inside of it. The smallest duck of them all hung from a silver chain with tiny diamonds all around him, and the words "I love you, little duck" were engraved on the back. The words caught me off guard so badly that I barely noticed the key tucked just behind it, but Kent explained before I could put my thoughts together or freak out about the admission.

"Don't care if it's fast. I mean it, Hadley. Don't know how it happened, but I fell for you in this month together, and even after the holidays, I'd like to see where this goes. Do you… want that… too?"

"Yes," I whispered breathlessly, flinging myself at him and kissing him like he'd just proposed. He might as well have, honestly. I'd have said 'yes' to that too, stupid or not, because something deep inside of me told me this was right. He was meant for me, but now that that particular truth was out in the open, my gift to him felt lame as hell.

"Um… well this is gonna be awkward. Your gift is in my purse. It's right behind you."

He turned to grab it and ripped the paper off to reveal a CD simply labeled "Santa Claus Is Coming… In Me," and a Christmas cracker filled with sex dice, kinky coupons, and a pair of edible panties. I blushed furiously, pissed I went sex-themed when he went utterly, devastatingly romantic, but it was too late to change course. "I had Stella burn us a copy of the footage from all the times we fucked in the store," I explained. "Figured we could watch it together sometime."

Kent's laughter soothed me in a way I didn't expect. "Fucking brilliant, Hadley. I—" He met my gaze and kissed me again, his hand finding home on the small of my back as he slid his tongue into my mouth. When he came up for air, I could see how much he loved it. "It's perfect. I can't believe I didn't even think to get those recordings. Thank you, luv. We're watchin' tonight."

"Why not right now? I've always wanted to have dirty sex while being watched by an audience of ducks," I teased, sliding off his lap and pulling my shirt off before dropping to my knees. "And for the record, Sir… I love you too. Let me prove it."

"I know you do," he replied with a grin, petting along my face so gently I somehow knew it meant he was about to wreck me. "You're a strange one, little duck… which makes you the only one for me."

I turned my cheek to nip his finger playfully and unbuttoned my jeans. "You're right. You've seen what happens when people forget that."

Kent huffed and pulled me to my feet. "Strip and then get back down. Need you naked for what's to come."

He pulled off his own shirt and watched me intently as I followed his orders, and the moment I sank back to my knees, he tugged my hair back so quickly I gasped. "So beautiful, baby girl." His hand slid down to cup my breast, swiping my nipple with his thumb before shoving it into my mouth. "Suck."

I shivered, wrapping my tongue around the pad of his thumb and sucking slowly, then a little messier as I locked eyes with him and let that intensity bring me to life. My hands were clasped firmly behind my back as I took that digit to the hilt, and even without looking at it I could see how hard his cock jumped in my peripheral vision.

He pulled his thumb out to free himself, sliding the head all along my lips before pushing inside, and I opened eagerly for him as he started to fuck my throat. I felt him pulling my hair and shoving deeper until my nose was pressed against his pelvis, and each thrust got harder until it actually started to hurt — but Kent didn't stop until his movements started to get erratic.

"Up. I need you."

Drool dripped down my chin as he picked

me all the way up off my feet to slide inside me, and all I could do was hold on and try to keep my balance as he lifted me higher and dropped me back down on his massive cock.

"Sir!" I screamed, digging my nails into the back of his neck as he railed me upright. "I'm—"

"Come for me, little duck."

It hit me so fucking hard that I jerked, squirting all down his legs and nearly slipping out of his grasp. In his haste to catch me, we pitched toward the tree, and it fell to the ground with a shattering jingle just as he laid me down to fuck me into the floor.

"Kent!" I gasped, rocking up desperately to meet each violent, brutal snap of his hips.

He covered my mouth, muffling any noise I might have made after yet another mind-blowing orgasm, but his movements started to falter a few seconds later. He groaned my name as he bred me, not moving his hand until long after my stomach was bloated with his come, and then he kissed me.

"I—I'm sorry about the tree," I said breathlessly. "That's my fault."

Kent shook his head and kissed the tip of my nose. "Don't worry about it, little duck. Think you can make it up to me next year?"

The thought of being with him next

Christmas — and all the Christmases after that — had a smile breaking across my face and my heart skipping a beat. "Yes, Sir," I said, kissing him again and lingering there as I traced the tattoos on his shoulders. "Promise."

He chuckled darkly as he plucked a piece of mistletoe from the fallen tree and held it above his cock. "Or, you can just start now," he offered.

My jaw dropped and I smacked him playfully, but we both knew I'd do whatever he asked me to and thank him for it afterward.

I *was* his slutty little elf, after all.

LOOKING FOR YOUR NEXT
OCTAVIA JENSEN READ?

VISIT
WWW.OCTAVIAJENSEN.COM

VISIT OCTAVIA JENSEN AT
www.octaviajensen.com
Or check her out on social media!
Facebook: Author Octavia Jensen
Instagram: @authoroctaviajensen
TikTok: @authoroctavtiajensen

Printed in Great Britain
by Amazon